Waiting for the Revolution

Cuba: The Unfinished Journey

Ten Days that Shook My Mind

Gustavo Gac-Artigas

Translated by Andrea G. Labinger

Havana, June 20, 2019

New York, June 30, 2019

Waiting for the Revolution
Gustavo Gac-Artigas
English Edition, September 2019
Translated by Andrea G. Labinger

Paperback:
ISBN: 978-1-930879-75-1
E-Book:
ISBN: 978-1-930879-77-5

Esperando la revolución
Spanish Edition, September 2019
paperback ISBN: 978-1-930879-74-4
Digital ed. ISBN: 978-1-930879-76-8
www.editorial-ene.com
Cover Picture: Muros en la Habana vieja, picture by
G.GA
Ediciones Nuevo Espacio

Printed in the United States of America

To my granddaughter Isabel,

with the hope that your dreams will transcend those of your grandfather and that you will create your own revolution.

¡Hasta la victoria siempre!

(Your incorrigible grandpa)

Fidel: *Let's go.*

Che: *We can't.*

Fidel: *Why not?*

Che: *We're waiting for Godot.*

Based on *Waiting for Godot.*

Samuel Beckett

When you receive this telegram, I will be on my way to Cuba. Notify my parents.

Chilean Postal Service, Valdivia, September 1968

I didn't have enough money to add a signature. I was thumbing my way, like dreams.

Journey's End

I closed my eyes and drifted off

drifted off only to awaken

I traveled in dreams, without a horizon, lost in the clouds, trying to make my mind go blank in order to write.

Cuba, 60 years after the dream, Cuba the imaginary, Cuba the lighthouse, Cuba the complement to May of '68 in my beloved Paris, to the Prague Spring on my beautiful Street of the Alchemists, Cuba the first free territory of Latin America, Cuba the cry that arose at student demonstrations in Chile, demanding that the doors to the university be opened to the world, or in support of a squatter district, or adding a cry of *Hasta la victoria siempre* to a *Ho Ho Ho Chi Minh, we will fight until the end.*

Arrival

It took me fifty years to arrive, with certain detours along the way, of course, from the time I left Valdivia, in southern Chile, in the year 1968.

And it wasn't revolutionary tourism, the obligatory visit of a left-wing intellectual of the era; everybody went, one after another; everybody had a photo taken with Fidel, a photo with Che, a photo to memorialize the occasion, even if later they would erase it from their memory, all of them, all but one, Gabo. But of course, Gabo had lived through one hundred years of solitude, and I, I never managed to grow the student revolutionary beard of the times, and I traveled by foot; I wasn't Wendy and I wasn't going to Castroland.

I had witnessed the invasion and death of the Prague Spring.

But let's get back to the present: what are fifty years in the life of a writer, what are sixty years in the life of a combatant, what are fifty years in the life of a dreamer?

I had trouble lifting my hand luggage into the overhead bin on the plane.

I've never traveled through life in a straight line, not even when I first learned to walk, but that's a different story, and I had already begun following the wrong curve in the road, the good one.

The first sensation – not thought – was of the burning air embracing my body, my pores opening to release many years of accumulated sweat, like an act of purification before entering Cuba.

I called on Marx, Lenin, Fidel, Che, Allende, the Orishás, Saint Barbara, and today, writing these lines, I realize that I had forgotten to call on the Party.

Maybe that was why I had never gotten there before, for that reason, and also because I had been in Prague in August of 1968.

Landing

The airport was a disappointment – in-significant, the same as any provincial airport, with no personality. It didn't sway to the rhythm of the tropical breezes, it didn't whisper the songs of Compay Segundo, its bureaucrats didn't flash warm smiles – in fact they didn't smile at all, or else they smiled police officers' official smiles.

The immigration officer took me back to memories of the RDA: dry, cold, steely gray eyes, defending access to the kingdom like a wall of immovable principles, arrogant, possibly because of the provenance of my passport, suspicious of what she saw.

"*Bienvenido*," she said, handing me back my passport and visa. I missed the customary *compañero*. I never thought that one day I would miss being called *compañero*, and yet I did. You can't always write a first page by forgetting the past, and my past pursues me.

A brightly lit corridor, bureaucrats chatting excitedly among themselves, ignoring us: Good? Bad? No, simply indifferent. How I would have loved to have been ignored in other times!

At the end of the corridor, before the space opened up, two tables and five white coats blocked the exit: health inspection! They changed the film on me, or rather (and this was hardly the same thing), a Resnais film suddenly flooded my memory, *Night and Fog*, cloudy and gray; this one, bright and shiny; that one, the barrier between life and death; this one, a protective barrier. Resnais' barrier led to life or death; the Cuban one led to my past or to my future.

The white coats blocking my way made me cough convulsively; five heads turned around, staring at me inquisitorially.

I went through.

I was in Havana.

Sensations

The second sensation was a leap into the past: haggling, haggling over prices, not because people were trying to cheat you, as you could read in the expressions of mistrustful tourists, but rather bargaining for the pleasure of making contact, of measuring yourself in the arena, knowing from the start that both parties would emerge triumphant, that defeat doesn't exist.

In Cuba no one pays the first asking price; what's more, to do so is considered offensive.

It all brought me back to Greece, where I haggled over everything, from a dish of octopus to a Comedy mask, Comedy always being cheaper and less respected than Tragedy. It brought me back to Tunis, where I haggled with the Hammamet Theater for one extra minute in which I, in turn, might bargain for love with La Bella entre las Bellas, in an eternal game that would change our lives minute by minute.

Cuba is a land of elections, not the one you might be thinking of – in that one the result is known from the start and makes no sense – I'm referring to life's important choices: a modern taxi or a shiny, old one for a postcard photo that doesn't reflect the driver's tragedy or dreams.

In order to make those important life choices eminently clear, we chose to stay at the small apartment of a young *cuentapropista*, or private entrepreneur, on Calle Peña Pobre in Old Havana, rejecting the luxury hotel that the conference offered us in Varadero, with its unlimited drinks and food, but where the sweet-and-sour odor of cheap liquor and the drunks stumbling from bar to bar on shaky legs, and the tables of endless, tasteless food where undistinguished dishes, pretentious plates of rice, chicken, and pork alternating with pork and chicken, tasted more sour than sweet, when the "all you can eat" was challenged by the humble, but proud "we eat whatever there is," and, just as when I was a child, and my mother said there was enough for everyone, we knew that to ask for more was to ask for less for my parents' plates, so too did we understand that the all-you-can-eat-and-drink policy in the luxury hotel meant less to eat for some Cuban family.

For its hidden, endless pleasure, I will always prefer the humble, delicious, curled-up shrimp to the haughty lobster, dry and stuffy, but smiling so as to charge more, that strumpet of the seas.

Through the taxi window we saw the scars left on the city by the destructive march of capitalism. What we didn't see was the construction of socialism. Years ago, I visited East Germany, where I observed the ruins of capitalism and the building of socialism: they were the show window of the new society, but something was missing: it was gray; it was sad; Berlin was monochromatic. Of course, it sat in the shadow of a wall, and walls, even defensive ones, are dangerous.

You never know where the enemy lurks.

In Cuba there was no gray: it was a painter's palette exploding under the sun; there were smiles; worn-out sandals beat a tired, but musical rhythm on the stones of the *Malecón*; palms and people swayed in the wind. It was a picture-postcard image, but for me, something was missing: I still hadn't found the soul of her people.

I lay down in bed to rest, closed my eyes, and marched into the past, afraid to awaken in the present.

At midnight I awoke from a dream in which Vargas Llosa was propositioning my wife, and she was flirting with him with a conspiratorial smile, like characters in a novel. I woke her: "It wasn't Vargas Llosa," she said to me sleepily, "it was García Márquez."

I spent the rest of the night awake, even though I had downed a couple of mojitos at La Bodeguita del Medio: you've got to make memories.

Dawn was breaking in Old Havana.

Day Two

Between our arrival and the next day, the pharmacy awaited me. Since everything in Cuba is recycled and nothing is wasted, Dr. José Martín Soro's pharmacy was now a bar, one that retained the doctor's sign and his name.

From the ancient shelf they took down a small, dark brown bottle, inside of which a thick, amber liquid kept ideas from evaporating.

They gave me three drops in a glass of mineral water, as there was no other kind, and the kind they did have evaporated before hitting the glass.

As the third drop fell, a black cloud crossed my path: the blockade.

The blockade is a crime.

We traveled on June 20; on the fifth of that month, the last authorized cruise ship had entered San Francisco pier in Havana, due to the tightening of external policies by the President of the United States. In the distance, the canticle of Brother Sun sank gradually below the horizon as tourists ran about aimlessly, abandoning the shoulders of the cruise ship, while the Cubans waited on the pier.

"Taxi? A Lulú-Marilú doll for the little girl? I've got the best in Havana, the real thing, not for tourists, mister."

The phrases and smiles remained silent, waiting, waiting for something to change.

"Change? Better than the official rate; the official rate never changes."

To blockade a people, to blockade nascent private enterprise, aspiring entrepreneurs, is a crime. Those who suffer are from the ranks of the people; they *are* the people. To block contact between human beings is inhumane, and everything that is inhumane is stupid; to isolate the isolated is to condemn them to live behind bars, stop them from dreaming, deny them sustenance for developing their thoughts, force them to think of a world of enemies and unyielding borders instead of an open, fraternal world where we all have rights, those same rights that are so often trampled by the powerful. To deny contact between two hands is to surrender that contact to weapons, be they ideological or those of the vultures who feed on confrontation.

What they couldn't blockade is the tongue of the Cuban people. No one can stop them; they loosen their tongues and it's like unleashing the storms from the very bottom of the Caribbean, to one side and another or to no side at all, with or without direction. They need to speak. I'm talking about those that have a tongue.

They make you seasick. I'm not kidding, I don't know why people offer you rum all the time when a simple conversation is sufficient, and just like with alcohol, when tongues are loosened, they rise up, toss you from one reality to another, ultimately making you realize that reality doesn't exist, and then, laughingly, abandon you to your fate.

I broke the blockade,

What I couldn't break is the internal blockage; that is more difficult and more dangerous. To blockade the blockage is a double crime.

I didn't break the blockade,

it's just that there are walls and there are walls.

And between both walls? I wondered.

Crossing the threshold of the first *paladar* I encountered, I replied to the "Hello, mister" in my beautiful language, *Hola, hermano.*

I ordered a dish of "whatever you have," but not a very big one; I had to leave room for my thoughts.

Cars

Old, gleaming, brightly painted colors where, ironically, red predominates, without catching the unwary tourist's attention. Laughing women, their blonde manes floating in the wind, allowed themselves to be driven up and down the *Malecón*, not realizing that more often than not, the ancient convertible has undergone as many plastic surgeries as they themselves have, and that its original, wrinkled ragtop has been hammered off by a clever auto body artist, transforming it into an object of desire for the tourists to ride back to the past, to their lost youth.

The films I watched at the Normandia Cinema in Chile, where the scratched celluloid transmitted its scars to the curtain when the house lights went off, returned today from the past on the streets of Old Havana.

I recognized the clothing, not the actresses: Marilyn, Jane, Joan, Bette, Zsa Zsa, Mae, and Marlene, adding her boozy voice. From the streets they were observed by the shadows of Anna, Gina, Simone, Katy, and – descending the staircase and closing the twilight of the myths – Gloria Swanson.

I grabbed a taxi.

I can't resist the call of celluloid love.

I Rolled through Havana

Streets, scars, parks, slogans disappearing from walls as if they were embarrassed. *Vas bien Fidel* (You're doing well, Fidel), says Camilo Cienfuegos to Fidel in Plaza de la Revolución. *Hasta la Victoria siempre* (Onward ever to victory) proclaims Che.

"Are you going to see La Roja play tonight?" asked a Chilean miner from Chuqui in Plaza de la Revolución. I told him that my last acting gig was in Chuqui on the night of September 10, 1973. He hugged me and we took some photos of ourselves as mementos, without names or faces or dates, to the memory of . . . and each of us remembered his own thing: I, the year 1973; he, who hadn't even been born then, wondering what the hell a Chilean was doing lost in that history and his ghosts when that night "La Rojita" was playing against the yellow team from Colombia.

"I hope we win," I said, just to say something. He was from Chuqui, and I didn't want to insult him by saying that John Lennon was waiting for me.

John was sitting on a bench in the square, motionless, his gaze lost in the distance. At his feet you could read: *You may say I'm a dreamer, but I'm not the only one.* The guard who looked after the park replaced his glasses so that he could read better; he didn't realize that the glasses had no lenses.

I wondered if all the glasses in Cuba came from the same optical shop.

John invited me to cross my legs and to join him in dreams.

Even the birds were quiet, and I swear, Cuban birds, like Cuban people, never stop singing.

I crossed the dream: diagonally across the park was the French Union Association of

36

Cuba: France, the land of my exile, the land that taught me love, the land that helped my wounds heal.

I smiled, approached the stairs that opened onto the Old World. In a doorway, the waitress said to me, "We've got the best mojito in Havana here."

Unmoving on his bench, John smiled ironically, while he furtively erased the part about the dreamer with his foot.

A cool breeze passed over the terrace, and in Havana, a cool breeze at midday is worth a fortune. Two musicians waiting, leaning against a wall. One of them, old enough to be historic, studied me with his gaze; the other, nearly as historic, asked the obligatory question: Where are you guys from?

After my reply, *Chile*, came the customary rejoinder: "Ah, Chile, a beautiful land," followed by a whispered comment to the more ancient man, "Where's Chile?"

Things went better for my wife, *from Puerto Rico*, followed by the all-too-familiar "Puerto Rico and Cuba, two wings of the same bird." Something similar happens in the U.S., but there they immediately drag *West Side Story* into the conversation.

The old cars began to arrive; they gaily circumvented Lennon, carrying young people, laughter, a quest for adventure, dreams that had no need of a reference point. They were neither better nor worse; they were other dreams, ones that didn't require reality.

The terrace filled up; we had brought them luck, so they brought me a bottle of rum, on the house, so that I would add whatever sacred liquid extract of sugar cane that would take me away from Paris and return me to that tropical Mass.

The historical musician traveled into prehistory and adapted "Guantanamera" to my story. I shed a few tears into my mojito, but in spite of the salt water dilution, it was still the best mojito in Havana.

"No," whispered Lennon. "The best mojito in the world is made from rum with history. Aged rum tastes better."

María stepped out on the dance floor, María, the most Latina of the young women who were laughing and dreaming beside us, María, the mother of the dance.

The party began. Even John started to dance and sing:

Ay, mamá,

Where do the singers come from,

For I find them charming,

and I want to meet them.

We come from the world,

that sovereign land,

we cross borders,

we come from nothingness

and we arrive without getting there.

Guantanamera,

Guajira Guantanamera,

our Chilean friend, it seems,

always caught the wrong flight

¡Ay, mamá!

There are cities you can never get to: Santiago de Chile, Havana. There are cities you can never get to, or where you always arrive too late.

¡Ay, mamá!

I got out quickly, as quickly as the Havana Club rum would let me. "Le temps des cérises" was fading. Even the steps of the staircase were swaying to the rhythm of the music.

My wife held me by the arm – just in case, she said lovingly – to keep my ideas from spilling out.

In the park, Yoko Ono tried to stanch the life that flowed from the love of her life, but John returned to his immobility and his dreams.

And he wasn't the only one.

Moors and Christians

A delicious cure for hunger, black and white accompaniment to a *ropa vieja* melting in my mouth and trying to escape between my teeth.

Moros y cristianos, Moors and Christians, the mixture, the *mestizaje*, Lulú-Marilú, a doll that's black on one side, white on the other, Africa and Europe, neither dominated nor dominating, Moors and Christians on a humble dish, equal in their task, a blend of colors, past and present, a humble future that appeases my hunger.

I hunger for affection, I hunger for feelings, I hunger for love, I hunger in my *ropa vieja*, my old clothes covering my old body as it surrenders to Moors and Christians.

"What would you like to drink?" the waiter jostled me from my musings.

"A daiquiri. No. Not a mojito, either." I had downed mojitos at breakfast. They had no beer. As for water, my stomach twisted, reminding me of the danger.

"A Cuba Libre!"

Fifty years later, a Cuba Libre, solitary and sad, looked at me ironically from the simple table. Even the rusty, hard metal chairs seemed to say: Park your backside here and excuse me for mentioning that fifty years ago we were both equally hard, but your backside was a little fuller then.

"It must have been because fifty years ago we were hopeful," I replied.

Illusions and Realities

The building was imposing. Peeling, its belly gutted, its veins open in the concrete, ripping apart, a piece of the ground destroyed; its roof let the starlight in. They weren't circular ruins, they were vertical, like the lovely, tall mahogany doors that led to the tenement where around fifty families lived. At the entrance, to the left, a tube poked out of the earth, cut off at ground level to hide its shame. It came from the depths of the island, a closed, black mouth, toothless as the smile of the Cuban people, an enigma-mouth that kept its secrets, denying itself to the lips of the thirsty.

"It's the water," the woman explained. "For months now we haven't had any. They say they're making repairs so it'll flow better and be less contaminated, which is an improvement, but it never gets here, which is why it smells bad, it never gets here. No, not every-where" – she anticipates my question – "not everything smells bad in Havana. We stinky ones are always the same – we smell of sweat, we smell of work, we smell of the burning sun that mercilessly dries up the water from our bodies."

As you can see, not everything is poetry.

The tube remained silent: a *compañera*, the neighborhood snitch of the new era, it stood watch. If the precious liquid appeared in its mouth, they connected a hose, brought a pump to speed its arrival, and started filling containers. It didn't get rid of the stink, but it calmed the people's thirst and it soothed their impotence.

A bittersweet rage began to compound the stench, and an angry stench tends to be a bad combination for those who govern.

In Plaza de la Revolución, Camilo Cienfuegos and Che Guevara held their noses.

Off to one side of the Plaza, in the government building, they closed the windows.

Were They Moors or Christians?

The building across the way had been refurbished as a hotel, clean, odorless, stretching its windows, its arms, toward reality, attempting to dip the feet of its enormous wooden doors in the water that drained from the black tube. Water had arrived, not for long, but at least for a few moments.

The shiny building licks its chops, and the odor, no matter how perfumed, swells up, sticks to everything, flows powerfully, passionately, it advances, advances implacably, like the people; the stench advances.

A few tourists emerged, laughing, leaving the beautiful doors behind.

Were they Moors or Christians?

Those facing me, those who showed me the way into their poverty, to their rooms, to their souls, looked at them, not with hatred, envy, or spite – they just looked at them, and that was enough.

Even my shoes ached.

Havana was growing smaller, as if the stone walls had shrunk: five people, a grandmother, her seven-year-old daughter, teenage daughter, and the teenager's seven-month old baby girl – her grandchild – plus her husband, three generations lived in one of the rooms of the ruins of grandeur, at the back of the patio, to the left, in a small space no larger than my cell in the Rancagua jail.

The difference is that I was forced to be there, and here they have no other choice; the difference is that we would laugh to chase away fear, while they smiled because, well, Cuban people smile. Which doesn't mean they accept their fate or are resigned to it; it means that in the tropics you won't survive if you live in bitterness.

The same can be said of jail.

They had divided the tiny room in half, crossways and lengthwise. Crossways they turned it into a duplex: in the upper part, near the roof, slept the young couple and their daughter; in the lower part was the grandmother-mother, not Neruda's *mamamadre*, but a young Mulatto woman who was a grandmother.

The first floor was divided in two. Against the wall was the small bed shared by the grandmother and her seven-year-old daughter; the other half served as a dining room or a living room or a game room, thanks to the TV, or as a space for guests when their nieces and nephews were dropped off there to be babysat.

The kitchen, stifling, hidden, clandestine, was fitted into a corner of the patio, the collective property of the conglomeration of fifty families.

The room was the individual part, the property of the family, the few miserable square feet that afforded them dignity. "No, it doesn't belong to the State, it's ours," and they proudly cast their gaze around their property. "It's ours, and we can exchange it if we find someone who wants it, and we can sell it; now we can sell it."

If you like, we can sell it to you; look at the marble – it's from Carrara.

Havana grew smaller on me and strangled my soul.

The ruined marble staircase assaulted one's eyes. Its brother, a block taken from the same quarry in Carrara, had been sacrificed to art and survived. The piece from which the staircase was carved had been surrendered to luxury and lust in long-lost times, and today, mortally wounded, it wounded the feet of the children who played on it.

The staircases of Havana, the marble flights of stairs of Havana, dirty, shiny, aggressive, the caress of a hooker unleashing desire through her feet, going up and down, escaping from the past, suffering in the present, and among them, in the infinite tomb, my future.

At night, in the Vedado neighborhood, food stands edged the shore: suckling pig, black beans and rice, the famous Moors and Christians, Cubans and the rest of the world, the rest of the Cuban world, all joined together by aroma, by hunger, not that one, the hunger of friendship.

Tongues were loosened.

A handsome couple approached us, proposing an exchange, not of ideas, but of partners. I thought of García Márquez.

Music vibrated in the air; the drinks were the people. They weren't tourism, they were blood and soul, they tasted different.

I got drunk.

My soul was dizzy with memories, vapors of yesterday that cloud my thoughts, but which bring back sensations. Night was falling over Havana.

I should have accepted the exchange.

On the Third Day He Rose from the Dead

It was at the intersection of Cuarteles and Monserrate. He crossed the street: "Good morning, I want to warn you that you can't change money outside of authorized locations."

He might be from Washington

He might be from Havana.

¡Ay, mamá!

Involuntarily I moved my feet, and La Bella, her hips.

"When you buy water," he went on, "make sure they open the bottle in front of you. Any other water isn't potable, but some bad citizens refill empty bottles."

He didn't say anything about the ice in the mojitos or daiquiris or ice pops.

"You can't buy cigars outside of authorized locations. Havana is the safest place in the world; I can guarantee that nothing will happen to you. I'm not a policeman, I'm from the Party."

As the song of the sea still resounded in my ears, I'm not sure if he said "I'm *from* the Party" or "I *am* the Party," or if there's a difference.

"Responsible for the security of this section of Old Havana" echoed in my ears. "We're deployed because many American agents have come here to spread lies about the revolution. They go around asking questions and talking."

I had just left one of my staircases, the building that justifies them, and the souls that inhabit them; all three had spoken to me. I felt like I was being observed. My staircases, my spirals, always have two directions, and I never know which way I'm going and where

Beatrice is. The marble exploded into a thousand pieces inside my head. Those who had opened their rooms and their hearts to me, regarded me sadly; the other guy, the Party member, with an expression that came from my past. On his chest he proudly displayed a little badge, that served as a sort of decoration. It read: "My name is Fidel." I was tempted to ask him, didn't he die?

I spoke, translating his language into modern times and adapting mine to ancient times, and hurled myself into the void and into my memories. The deeper I plunged into the past, the more I distanced myself from reality, the happier my *compañero* became: he even embraced me – my body, not my ideas.

If not, I'd really have been screwed.

I returned, I returned to the time of hope, to the triumph of the revolution, to Fidel's entrance into our lives, the living Fidel, that is, not the little badge. In my journey to the past, I found him and could speak with him – not with Fidel, but with him, the Party.

He took my picture in front of the headquarters of the Vilma Espín Federation of Cuban Women – a sign of progress. He told me that there were very few Party officials, that the admission process was very selective, that one had to prepare, that they had certain privileges. To prove this, he gave me half of the Havana cigars that the Party had given him, 25 of them, so that the smoke of its principles would surround me.

It was a land of *santería* and principles.

"See you around, *compañero*," he said as he walked away.

I removed one step from my staircases.

"Ciao, *compañero*," I replied, as I hid the step where he couldn't find it.

And it was from Carrara, I said to myself with a hint of nostalgia.

Sculptures

Cold, marble women with warm curves, silent women concealing a cry of love, women with bodies caressed by the sculptor's hands, their flesh wounded by the chisel, their souls hidden, waiting to surrender to him, to her, if only for five minutes; in five minutes, life is eternal.

"She was buried in the garden, on the patio of the Conde O'Farrill mansion on Calle Cuba; she turned up when we were remodeling."

The first mansion was expropriated, then converted into offices and later residences for certain families. Then it became uninhabitable, and finally they decided to refurbish it and turn it into a luxury, five-star hotel, with 35 rooms, we were told. "As you see, the revolution marches on."

"What happened to the families?"

"Remember where you come from, or have you already forgotten that you crossed the street?"

Rescued from the depths of the earth, the sculpture was in the middle of the entry hall, resting seductively, with a distant gaze, her legs crossing or spreading, blocking or insinuating, dispensing desire or compassion, depending on whether it was the Count touching her or his slaves devouring her with their eyes.

She had scars on her body, someone had raped her, *#metoo* could be heard emanating silently from her lips. The beautiful marble staircase emerged from between her legs and rose toward the rooms; scars remained scattered along the steps.

New wounds opened within those rooms.

In the front building, the vertical ruins, the wounds struggled to climb the first step. Conversations escaped through the holes in the walls. Just like in Prague, back in '68, in Old Havana tongues had come untied, without shame, without censorship, without fear: brave, defiant, hopeful and without provocation, and if the security guard was listening, who cares – or rather, let him listen, so much the better.

Storms incubate, they inCUBAte, if it's true that ancient languages, on both sides of the ocean, disappear into the bottom of the sea, lose their place in the present and become mud, sterile mud dissolving in one's thoughts.

Soon you'll see!

Ay, mamá, I want to know

Where the speakers come from,

For I find them charming,

and I want to meet them

61

with their hesitant speech

and I want to learn.

They might be from Havana,

that sovereign land,

they're from the hillside

they sing on the plains

soon you'll see

soon you'll see

soon you'll hear them.

I walked away singing

singing the past

singing the present

singing the future

Soon you'll see!

Soon they'll see!

I felt like a *Habanero* in quest of happiness.

At Plaza de la Revolución someone was selling cotton balls for plugging up ears; and yet, in the past they listened, even in the midst of the sound of gunfire they listened, from the Sierra Maestra, they listened, and the din rose and they came down, and they embraced.

When did they plug up their ears?

All of them?

Some of them?

Mamá, I want to know . . .

On the sea, the cotton balls dissolved in the boat people's ears; in Old Havana, the decibel level of thought was turned up.

On the Third Day, Ring the Bell...

...accompanied by a Havana Fresh.

Cross the bar, ring the bell three times, three rings only, and make a wish. Don't tell anyone, so that it will come true. Then go up to the bar and order a Havana Fresh: it has three colors, the colors of the flag.

It was Che's bar.

I wonder what Ernesto "Che" Guevara ordered, and if his wish came true or if he told it to Fidel.

Yemayá didn't give me the answer, even though I had just come out of the Museum of Fine Arts, where I went to chat with Wilfredo Lam.

At the entrance, a ship greeted me, a ship on the floor made of small crafts, of shoes recovered from the sea, of dolls, interrupted dreams, headless dreams, an empty wallet, scattered corpses, hope's castaways, the spoils of humanity, hundreds of boat people plunged into the sea of despair.

The author's name had been ripped off, swept away, perhaps, by another storm. In one corner, a broom waited for the signal to start cleaning.

I brought the ships and the dead back in my heart, till death do us part.

I climbed another step; Wilfredo was waiting for me.

Demons escaped from the heads of the figures in his paintings; demons populated my own head; demons danced in the air, inviting me to abandon reality and open myself up to fantasy.

A female demon held a baby on her lap: the Pietà? Maternity? The baby had horns;

motherly love suffused the gallery; my demons sought a moment of rest, a moment of mercy.

Serpents, lances, knights, horses with teeth bared, whinnying their agony to the heavens, Guernica reborn in the slaves' pain, intermingled paint brushes challenging death, demanding the right to live.

On the first floor, the waves, the breeze, and the visitors' footsteps erased all traces of the boat people; the floating corpse of a little girl who returned from the Beyond without a head; Wilfredo and Pablo's horses whinnying their pain to the world; the little girl, the headless little girl: even that right had been denied her.

The remains continued to float: was this slavery? Was it socialism?

The music tormented my ears as I tried to summon the final words from those lips that history had sealed.

On the second floor, Fidel mustered everyone to the ten-million-ton sugar cane harvest. "We didn't reach our goal, but it wasn't a defeat; we were very poor and we believed, my parents believed; when the machetes rested, they made love in the cane fields and conceived me; I am the fruit of the ten million; it wasn't a defeat; sometimes I feel guilty for not believing as they do, for thinking that if they hadn't stopped to make way for love, they might have reached ten million. Who knows? It's just that they were so poor," explained the woman who watched over the gallery, smiling at me with her toothless mouth.

I'm about to end my] third day at the Buena Vista Social Club.

"Another daiquiri, *compañero*."

"One CUC to buy a copy of *Granma*, just one CUC, it's to help me eat, *compañero*."

One step forward

one step back

loosen your hips

let yourself go

the music will bring rhythm back to your blood.

Don't look at your feet

let yourself go

another daiquiri, goddammit

for I'm drowning in memories.

Buena Vista Social Club

"The best show in Havana, the best interpreters of Cuban music, the classics: put your hands together for one of the vedettes of the Tropicana."

I was transported: beautiful, in a dress as blue as the sky that covers Cuba, like the sea that bathes Cuba, like the blue of the flag that waves over the head of Martí's statue in Plaza de la Revolución. Clinging to her body like a food rations card – four eggs, a quarter kilo of chicken – her arms moving to the rhythm, her hips overtaking her arms, shiny, silvery high-heel shoes, "Let's hear it for Mayra Mitchell."

The Tropicana came back to life before our eyes; she sang, danced, and strutted up and down the catwalk, offering up the old, timeworn dream; 80 years came flooding back from pre-revolutionary days, 60 years from the moment of the Revolution; love and myths flooded the room with their sweet-and-sour fragrance.

¡Ay, mamá! She proudly displayed her breasts, sixty years, and they pointed to the future, to the past, and to the sky. *Soy cubana,* the kettledrums echoed, *Soy cubana,* the trumpet proclaimed to the air, *Soy cubana,* cried the next vedette, today an adolescent, *Soy cubana* sang the Chilean women, the Argentines, the Puerto Ricans in the audience.

Soy cubana, the headless doll admonished me, as she floated in the Caribbean.

I opened the windows; this was the kingdom of music, and I needed to embalm my body with song.

Tula's room has caught on fire

She fell asleep

and didn't blow out her candle.

In Old Havana things are upside down,

everything is upside down,

there's no water

and nobody put out the candles.

¡Ay, mamá! What happened?

The Malecón

The sea, I love the sea, the sea enfolds me, the sea opens my horizons, caresses me, drowns me. In an ocean of multitudes, it allows me to be an island and be singular, and being singular allows me to dream and be a multitude.

Bodies of young lovers sitting on the eroded rock, a soft bed for new loves, their gaze lost on the horizon, the future, or the habitual.

The Malecón, Havana's seaside promenade, encounter of water and stone, a battle since time immemorial, water carving stone, stone resisting, water slowly advancing, gentling, making its way, stone still resisting, surrendering, allowing itself to be penetrated while the lovers watch.

Who will the victor be?

Day Four: The Open University of Havana

Consummate professionals, the Cubans: for every address they are asked, even if it doesn't exist, and in order to make the human contact last longer, they spew out (may they forgive me) an avalanche of answers. The streets vanished from our view: the *vista* wasn't *buena*. Yes, it was social, but it wasn't a club; it was pain and the new profession.

I found the university on the street, all of them professionals, true, false, who wants to know, sometimes they were professions that adapted themselves to the victim, or rather the questioner, sometimes they were genuine: a lawyer, today a waitress; a geologist, today extracting minerals of small change from the speaker's pockets.

Speaker isn't the right word – listener, perhaps – that is, if one knows how to listen.

"We are the safest city in the world; the university is free", and it's true that people study; what we don't know is what for. For the future, to save or waste time, maybe thinking about the past, maybe about the future, maybe about the fact that time passes more easily when one dreams, when one learns, when . . .

After socialism, the first phase, the inferior stage of the dream, the time of sacrifice, comes the building of communism, the superior stage of the dream, where there will be no more social classes or private ownership of the means of production, where each will receive according to his needs.

Equality, divine treasure, Lenin repeated. In Old Havana people stood in line, ration cards in hand. There was fish for sale, free commerce of fish, one fish per family, the fish head for bachelors, the tail for old folks.

And after communism, what? I wondered, joining the line for eggs.

"Capitalism," responded a voice from the university of the streets, "and then we'll start all over again. The Revolution is permanent, as Trotsky said; it's eternal. Want a taxi? I'll take you."

And the lawyer started to pedal his taxi-bike.

I come from the theater,

I am the theater

And cardboard sets annoy me: I ran across them in Bulgaria, in the GDR, in France, and in Chile.

In the United States they're made of plastic that looks like cardboard.

Progress?

The university exists to be possessed, to be embraced, to be changed through love, to break down barriers, to say no, I don't want to repeat anything, I want to be a soloist, not a chorus, I don't want to be a model, I want to be a wild wind, a river that bursts its banks, I want to be a stormy sea and never reach the shore, your shore, society's shore; I want to be a castaway trying to learn, so that tomorrow when I reach my shore, someone will destroy it and return me to the stormy waters of life.

"Where to?" insisted the taxi-bike lawyer. He was in a hurry, like the shoeshine man in Elia Kazan's *America, America.* "There's nothing deceptive about pedaling; I earn my living through my own effort, I wipe my sweat with a threadbare towel, and as I pedal I review the Roman Code. I wipe my sweat and pedal. Because of the heat, nobody realizes I'm not really sweating, and I slyly wipe my eyes with the towel. I go along the seashore and sneak a glance at the horizon."

The headless doll whispers to him from the bottom of the sea: "there you'll pedal, too, and wipe your sweatless sweat, casting furtive glances at the sea, but in the opposite direction. "

"Need a taxi?" I heard once more. "At least give me a peso to get something to eat, help me out a little and I'll take you to a *paladar*, the best in Old Havana; if you make a reservation, they'll give me a dish of *moros y cristianos,* my only meal of the day."

I paid for the reservation, but I didn't go back. I had lost my appetite.

"Let me walk with you. You know how much I earn? You think somebody can live on that, somebody can eat on that, somebody can laugh on that? I live with my mother, she's sick, I invite you to see how I live, come up and meet my family. One peso and seventy-five *centavos*, with that I'll buy a quarter chicken, thanks, thanks very much. I'm not begging.

It's out of necessity. Come upstairs and have a coffee."

I took it without sugar.

Those who didn't earn a doctorate ask for money while sitting in the street; those with a master's degree tell stories; the doctors serve as guides."

Cuba is indeed very safe. No one will attack you, but they'll attack your thoughts and feelings.

"Help me out, one peso to get some food."

And they're not beggars, I swear; they can't be beggars. Maybe they're just asking for one peso's worth of understanding, one peso's worth of friendship, one peso of revolution. Cubans have dignity, I assure you.

"A copy of *Granma* for a peso, help me," asked the newspaper vendor.

I wonder if they're selling *El Siglo* for a peso in Chile...

"Help me, *compadre*, give me a peso to buy her a copy of *Granma*."

El Siglo? That was the last century.

Goin' to Varadero

On the fifth day, I left for Varadero, the most beautiful beaches in Cuba, a tourist paradise. I left Old Havana behind, though you can't leave old Havana behind; you carry it in your soul.

At breakfast time, a 21-cannon salute echoed in my ears. My body trembled with the memory of other cannon fire, but this time it was a tribute.

Proudly I went out to the balcony to greet the people who would gather in response to the cannons' call, the Cubans' love of literature, I thought. The geologist who served breakfast summoned me back to reality: "Come, your coffee's getting cold, and don't be afraid: it's not a landing. Today is Maceo's anniversary – that's the reason for the shots."

I picked up my suitcase, the computer, and a printed copy of my conference presentation. Downstairs, Yuri, a modern astronaut in his '55 Ford, awaited me. The agency had assured me that it was an air-conditioned taxi, and it was true. Yuri rolled down the car's four windows, and the air circulated merrily among the passengers.

As he loaded the car, Yuri recognized a fellow proletarian internationalist, and said to me, "Don't tell them how much I charged you. I charged the two Swiss girls double."

I am of the people

I am the people

and together with the people

I always stand.

I kept the secret.

Yuri flew lower than his namesake, but he dreamed of flying above the stars; on the earth, before our eyes, the highway unrolled to the rhythm of Yuri's tongue.

To our left, the sea; to our right, endless rows of agave, green gold, a plant that to this day is unraveled and its fiber used to make bags and rope, good-quality rope, the kind that doesn't break, the kind that ties up dreams. And sometimes, with luck, you get a hammock to numb your dreams to sleep.

"The car is mine; I pay fees and they allow me up to twelve trips to the airport to pick up passengers. Twelve per month – can you imagine? Even in Cuba a month has more than twelve days, and what am I supposed to do with the rest? Sometimes clients returning to the island call me, and I can't go to pick them up, and I pay fees, and the fees are for the month, the kind that have thirty days.

"You can't progress like that, and I want to progress. I fix my car, I wash it, I repair it, and when I can't find spare parts I'm stuck, and the month has thirty days, thirty days, stuck or working, the month doesn't give a damn, but it matters to my house, my kids, my stomach.

"Luckily you're going to a hotel I'm allowed to enter. There are others where I'm not allowed to pull up to the door, and my passengers are the same, and I need to work and it embarrasses me to tell them I can only drive up to here; they won't let me inside because they think I'll pick up someone for the return trip for less money. I want to live, too; I want to progress, too.

"I'm not political; I've got my feet planted on the ground, not like that other Yuri who went up in space, spinning around the earth."

And, laughing like a good Cuban, he added: "Though maybe way up there, far from reality, you can make better progress. And if you'll permit me a joke, they call our new president a TV with no remote control," and he burst out laughing on the way to Varadero, to its fantasy beaches.

He hit the gas.

Shoot the Piano Player

The conference began: I was to read on the first day about my own writing. I trembled: in my paper I spoke of censorship, and I knew censorship all too well. I had no idea how my audience would react.

I had stopped by the market; the tomatoes were prohibitively expensive. Then I calmed down and was glad that I had defiantly worn a white shirt. White shirt, red shoes, just in case.

I talked, I talked about creativity, I talked about the sources of creativity, I quoted Ai Weiwei, a Chinese dissident; in a country where one pays for being a dissident, one pays with silence, a thundering silence that smothers one's voice.

I talked about Evstuchenko, who was condemned to the editorial wastelands; doors were closed to him; his readers' minds were opened. Twenty-six years later, his voice emerged again from the depths, every bit as vibrant as when it emerged in '68 in the amphitheater of the southernmost university on the planet, in Valdivia, Chile.

There are moments when what lies beneath is what shines brightest, when darkness illuminates, when artificial light is blinding, when certainty doesn't exist, when doubt is the polestar.

I talked about all of that as the shadows enfolded me, and yet I was happy, the veil of the temple was torn in two; a girl in the front row smiled at me; sitting beside her, my wife warned me: "Be careful, remember Vargas Llosa."

Wasn't that García Márquez? I was struck by doubt, and to hell with the literary allusions – this time I want certainty.

Afterward, everyone embraced me; I saved my skin. Once more they hadn't understood, or else they understood me all too well. In magical Cuba, behind every saint hides an *orishá*.

As night falls, an image, face down. Oscar Alberto Martínez, age 45. Around his neck, a tiny arm clings to the security of her father, face down, a little body half hidden in her father's undershirt, half naked in her father's undershirt, subject to life, to death,

Giddyup, Papá,

Giddyup, Daddy,

we're almost there,

it was Angie Valeria

23 months old

the ladies ride at the walk

the gentlemen ride at the trot

and the horsemen at the gallop

gallop, gallop

the poor

swimming toward death

at the gallop,

gallop,

gallop,

the current sweeps them away

they were crossing the Río Grande

The bodies appeared, face down, inches from the dream of a better life. They had waited two months for their papers, requesting asylum at the border between Mexico and the United States. They managed to arrive from El

Salvador; they grew desperate, they wanted to celebrate the baby's second birthday in the Land of Opportunity.

They tried to swim across the Río Grande.

Angie Valeria slipped her little arm around her father's neck to hug her savior. The other Savior, El Salvador, the land where she was born, was awash with violence.

At the bottom of the water, in the depths of the river, two little girls came together, the headless Cuban child who appeared floating in the Caribbean, and Elvira, the Salvadoran, her face stuck to her father's back, both children headless, both of them with severed dreams.

23 months, 23, nearly the same age as my granddaughter.

One of them escaped violence, the other, non-violence; one dreamed, the other dreamed; both might have played with my granddaughter one day, all three of them saying *It's my turn, I'm next,* it's my turn to dream.

My granddaughter gliding down the slide in the playground; Elvira clutching the security offered by her father; the headless Cuban girl, her body in Havana, her head and her dreams sailing somewhere, waiting for Charon to join them back together.

It's my turn to dream.

I cried.

"It's your turn to cry, Grampa,

Cry.

Feel better now?"

Night was falling in Varadero; night reigned in the United States; hope drowned along the border.

¡Ay mamá!

Where do the bodies come from

For I find them . . .

Second Day in Varadero

Brevity was the order of the day at the conference: in three minutes learning, teaching, thinking – sorry – teaching, learning, transmitting, transmitting, transmitting questionnaires that don't ask questions, ideologies that don't differ from the overriding ideology, the established order. Time passed, time doesn't rewind; the quality and long-sought equality, fade away.

And still they search, converse, interchange ideas, take advantage of any crack to peer beyond the wall; poetry slipped between the seats; the occasional commissar stood watch, the word emerged, sparkling but dense, so that they might not discover it. Potent and malleable, the word was a contradiction in their minds.

There was hope.

Man lives from hope.

Luckily the daiquiris were unlimited.

Matanzas

City of bridges. To get there, we crossed the highest bridge in Cuba. I wondered what the lower ones are like, but never mind, each one is as high as it needs to be. The important thing is that it's a bridge you can cross, which unites, which can be crossed in any direction, and which, if you fall, doesn't do your thoughts much harm.

Cuba is a constant surprise; a city of bridges, a dream, a message to humanity, a song of hope; a city of dreams in a world where the President of the United States dreams of building barriers to prevent the entrance of those fleeing violence; where another president, in Venezuela, blocks bridges to prevent the escape of those fleeing from hunger. On both sides are the bridge-destroyers, those who deprive a bridge of its *raison d'être,* the kings of barriers, those who deep down want to prevent the entry of ideas, the circulation of thought hidden beneath the hunger, beneath the fear.

In Matanzas, on the other hand, thought grows, strolls around the historic city, bounces off its walls, turns into paper, turns into images on the paper, turns into letters on the paper, turns into love slipping from the paper.

Mamá, I want to know

where the writing comes from

For I find it moving

and I want to make it my own

On the second floor, students read their work beneath the protective gaze of their professors; on the second floor, professors observed their students beneath the watchful shadow of the *compañero* who would summarize things, draw previously written conclusions, just like the conclusions of the congresses of yesteryear.

The blonde from Varadero was in the audience. She had earned another gold medal, and Olympically began her doctoral program. She smiled at me.

I was surrounded, surrounded by handmade books, not more than 200 copies, illustrated by artists, one after another, with love, images and words, open windows, open doors, the world coming in and going out, "La Vigía," the watchtower, watching to make sure no one would close a single door.

Downstairs they read my poems. My manuscript remained behind; it left me in order to escape through the windows and doors and emerge into the world.

Two hundred in single file, one by one, from the massacre, off to conquer the world.

Thanks.

Radio Rebelde

They stopped me in the middle of the staircase. I stood balanced between two moments in time.

"I'm a correspondent from Radio Rebelde; I'd like to interview you."

The words echoed in my ears like heavenly music: *Just like you, just like you, I listen to Radio Moscow*, with the latest news from Chile in her battle against the dictator. In my ears echoed the first four notes of Beethoven's Fifth Symphony, *da-da-da-duuuum*, dot-dot-dot-dash, V for victory in Morse code, followed immediately by messages to the guerrillas in France, direct from London, *Radio London here, Frenchmen talk to Frenchmen*, till the day they read the poet's words, D-Day. In my ears echoes of Radio Rebelde, a station founded by Che, *Radio Rebelde here, the voice of Sierra*

Maestra, transmitting *news throughout all of Cub of Fidel and the guerrillas' advance.*

In my ears, in the midst of gunfire, echoed Radio Magallanes: *Surely this will be the last opportunity for me to address you . . . workers of my country, I have faith in Chile and its destiny.*

The Second Declaration of Havana echoed in my ears, Fidel addressing the Cuban people and the world: *For this great humanity has said "enough!" and has begun to march.*

The film faded from my mind, and I saw myself delivering the Third Declaration of Havana. I had even bought myself a beret with a red star, but this was Matanzas, not Havana, and it was me, not Fidel. After 16 minutes they took away my microphone, just as I was about to unroll the revolutionary lyrics.

In Plaza de la Revolución, the *compañeros* started to take down the platform.

How I Learned the True Story of Che's Death

I was walking along Calle Obispo on my way to have a daiquiri at the Floridita Bar. The *jineteras,* latter-day hookers, attacked my mind and my pockets; I couldn't tell if they were the descendants of the ones who gave Cuba its fame as the whorehouse of Latin America, those who were liberated when Fidel entered Havana, or if they were the product of sixty years of Revolution, or a mirage of capitalism defeated.

On one side of the street, bookstores halted the attack, paper castles across time, the smell of fresh ink and mold, pages that had escaped censorship, hidden pages that emerged from the foam of the waves, letters marching slowly, allowing themselves to be stroked by the avid reader's fingers, paragraphs that tenderly regarded the inevitable

Che posters, which escaped from the walls only to die at the bottom of tourists' suitcases; not travelers, tourists:

wily death.

More than one book shuddered at the possibility of falling into the wrong hands, illiterate fingers that would mark its first pages, but even an illiterate finger is a pleasure, they comforted themselves.

In the distance, a writer shuddered. The chill of the daiquiri rose through his nose up to his brain, avenging needles that drove off evil thoughts.

Election time again. Cuba is a country of elections, of choices, I repeated to myself, looking at the bill from which Che stared at me. From my hand, Che looked at the contents of the book – novel, poetry, history? No, not history; that strolled up and down the streets of Old Havana, slipped along the walls, slid down the marble staircases, was caught up by the bald wiring that brought light to the squalid dwellings, extinguished the dreams of the eldest, illuminated the dreams of the headless girl.

History hurt my bones and my soul.

A voice brought me back from my musings: "I was there; I was a witness; I'm going to tell you the true story of how Che died."

The voice wasn't the right age, but it doesn't matter: I'm used to chatting with ghosts, and ghosts are ageless, moving endlessly through history and time.

"Che was betrayed. I went to Ñancahuazú, Bolivia, to the schoolhouse in La Higuera; at the door I heard, 'Say hello to Papá.'"

Papá was Ramón, Ramón was Che, the orphans were us.

"They betrayed him," the witness went on.

I thought of Mario Monje, secretary of the Bolivian Communist Party, who refused to give Guevara logistical support because of a "who's in charge here" attitude, at a time when the one in charge was in cold, distant lands. He refused to support him, knowing that his refusal meant death. After turning Che down, Mario went on playing the piano.

Mario's arm dried up, and the symphony remained unfinished.

"It wasn't him," said the voice. "It was a Cuban, his best friend."

I trembled: the black legend of the Caribbean; Fidel, because of "who's in charge here."

"No, it was his best friend. He walked into the room where Che was resting, pistol in hand."

John Wayne! John Wayne insinuated himself into the film. I love gunslinger movies.

What I don't like is when the hero dies halfway through.

"No, it wasn't Wayne. I like him, too," said the Cuban guy. "It was his best friend – he aimed at him and said: 'I've come to kill you.'"

"Che burst out laughing. 'Put down the M2; the autoloader might go off.'"

"The best friend looked him in the eyes. 'They ordered me to kill you.' He closed his eyes and fired."

Che died with his eyes open, uncomprehending.

The voice faded in the distance, limping down Calle Obispo and disappearing into the crowd.

I ran after the echo so as to see his face and untangle the mystery of Che's second death.

Sitting on the sidewalk, an old man, Mario Terán, with one red eye and one eye blank, regarded me ironically. "One CUC, one CUC for the true story of how Che died".

"He closed the door as he left," a *jinetera* whispered in my ear. "He was a good friend."

Or might it have been to keep Che's spirit from following him?

The Tunnel of Time

3-4-8 Tejadillo, at the corner of Habana and Aguiar, a narrow doorway, navy blue, gave way onto a dark corridor, an endless leash that disappeared in the shadows. From inside came a voice. I trembled.

"Come in, there's no obligation."

I did have an obligation, but I couldn't say what it was. The voice emanated from the shadows, crossed in front of me and continued along Aguacate toward La Subida del Ángel.

A sharp whistle pierced my thoughts. "Come in, we're a community of painters. This is our gallery."

I left my fears at the entryway, resting against one of the beams of the wooden door.

I entered, my fears following my footsteps.

Halfway inside, a tiny figure crossed my path; it was the owner of the sibylline voice. It wasn't his fault; he was missing several teeth. My back was hurting; behind me, the first voice cut me off. He never came out.

"We are six painters." Six, who hung their work on walls, in a corner, on the roof, among the spider webs. I passed from one to another, from one to another without much interest, until . . . perched on a chair, dusty, a reminder of a familiar place, Putaendo, an engraving similar to those of Pedro Lobos that I had seen in my childhood.

Lobos, who died when I was starting out on my journey.

Hands of the people, faces of the people, soul of the people, large eyes of my people. Faces crafted one by one, carved into the wood, penetrating the heart of the oak, inked one by one, transferring their imprint to the humble sheet of paper; these were the faces of my people, reflecting hope, revealing their blemishes, their alcoholism, engraved forever the traces of injustice that they could not erase from their faces, or from the withered hands of Lobos' mother, a rural washerwoman, hands of my people, hands that survived in the hands of her son Pedro, yes, he who distributed bread and wine and painted kites at the country festivals in Putaendo.

I picked it up respectfully and sat on the dusty chair.

"It was made by a Chilean," said the sibylline voice, "like you."

Immediately his tongue loosened:

"I don't understand why Allende didn't distribute arms to the people. In Valparaíso, we Cubans had two ships with weapons, and the ambassador called Allende and told him: We're ready to unload and distribute them to the kids, the *cabros;* that's how he spoke to him, in plain Chilean, so there would be no doubt whatsoever, and Allende said no. I don't know why he said no."

The voice whispered, "Maybe he wanted to avoid a massacre." His voice wandered. "I'm a painter and a poet, and I've traveled around the world, living just like here, in any way possible; the important thing is to dream."

His voice pleased me. He was worldly, and he had read beyond borders.

"There are other Chileans, there were lots of Chileans, some still remain, others left, others we never laid eyes on again, Chileans are like ghosts – they appear from time to time. I don't understand; we could have given them weapons," he insisted.

My voice played ghost; it didn't reply. I had learned to play ghosts, *peek-a-boo.*

"One guy made films. We held meetings to pay for the material. He was a fisherman –

don't get Biblical on me. This one fished at the Malecón, with a rope, like the Cubans. He prepared the fish Chilean style, and at the meeting he passed them out without charging; everybody chipped in something for the material, so that he could finish his film about the fishermen in southern Chile, something like the loaves and fishes but without the bread.

"I never saw the film," said the voice.

"We'll expect you tomorrow. We're going to bring the Chilean and have some nice bottles; Chileans make good red, and a nice bender wakes up the past, and maybe you'll be able to explain to me why Allende wouldn't let us distribute the weapons; we were waiting for his order."

I played ghost. History doesn't repeat itself, and they did give me a weapon, but it had no bullets.

Riddles

Che died for you.

And you? Who will you die for?

Rum Rum

he went up north

I don't know when he'll be back

May Violeta Parra forgive me, but that was the name of the restaurant, and that's where we had our last supper in Old Havana. A group of musicians sang in the doorway.

La Scala in Paris

La Peña de los Parra in Chile

Peña Pobre Street in Havana

boleros in the street

boleros in my hands

boleros caressing La Bella's hands

boleros in our eyes

that's why doors were opened to them

as they passed, they thanked us

in reply

in the middle of a *ropa vieja* they sang a cha-cha-chá

that I had used in a play in Paris,

for each *cha*, a zap of current

then the Martians came

and they came dancing *ricachá*

richachá, ricachá, ricachá

as they call the cha-cha-chá on Mars

followed by boleros

suddenly,

in one second,

without warning,

The Basin*

See the basin, how it sloshes

how the water sloshes in the basin

the basin of my years of exile in Paris

in Old Havana,

what madness!

How history sloshes in the basin

I joined in the song.

And Violeta?

That dear little angel

went straight up to heaven.

*La Batea, a song by Cuban composer Toni Taño. The version by Chilean musical group Quilapayún (1971) became an international hit.

The Artisans' Workshop

Omar returns from the shadows,

he sells us three serigraphs

we talk

and then he gives us all we want

proudly he shows us

a picture of his son

principal dancer with the Kansas City Ballet

in his arms

in the air

in infinite space

the prima ballerina

his girlfriend

and the waters kept churning,

the sharks lying in wait

and the bodies being devoured

but

just like Nureyev, someone makes the 90-mile
leap

90 miles or else

drowns ten inches from shore, from the
dream,

in the Río Grande

And in Kansas City, in *Swan Lake* he shakes

and the public, entranced, sees a dancer

who sometimes moves his hips to the rhythm

of Santiago de Cuba

¡Ay, mamá!

where are the dancers from

for I find them attractive

and I want to take them home with me

¡Ay, mamá!

He was trained by Alicia Alonso and danced throughout the world, and the world turned out to be too small for him; he needed to breathe, he needed infinite space to levitate, and once in the clouds, that beloved angel, he looked at his father, Omar, who, at the workshop in Old Havana, proudly told anyone who wanted to listen, my son is the principal dancer of the Kansas City Ballet.

No one believed him, no one, till he showed them the photo in which, smiling the same smile, but with sadness in his eyes, his son appeared, steering his boat 90 meters in the air, the father sitting on the Malecón.

The Last Night I Spent with You

On the last night, a storm, lightning, and sparks lit up Old Havana. Havana doesn't let anyone leave: it rips itself apart, it tears you apart, sets you aglow, makes you shiver, screams at you from its heart: Don't forget me, remember: fifty years ago, I was your first love.

Sixty years later the dream was fulfilled; they destroyed it and returned us to our starting point.

We entered times of sadness.

Day Ten: Spirals

I traveled back, took the plane; it was a round-trip dream; I closed my eyes, and parodying Neruda, exclaimed: Cuba in my heart!

When I opened them, a beggar was walking between the rows of cars, holding up a sign:

I am homeless

I am hungry

any help is good

God bless you

I was in America.

Havana, June 2019

New York, July 2019

¡Ay, mamá!

Gustavo Gac-Artigas is a Chilean writer, poet, playwright, actor, and theatre director. A corresponding member of the Academia Norteamericana de la Lengua Española (ANLE), his poetry has been published in the *RANLE* (ANLE's literary review), *Enclave* (CUNY), *Multicultural Echoes* (CSU-Chico) *Viceversa*, and other literary magazines. In 1989 he received a Poetry Park award (Rotterdam) for his short story "Dr. Zamenhofstraat," and in 2018, his novel *And All of Us Were Actors: A Century of Light and Shadow* (2017), translated by Andrea G. Labinger, was first runner-up for the 2018 International Latino Book Award. As a fiction writer he has published: *Tiempo de soñar* (1992) *¡E il orbo era rondo!* (1993), *El solar de Ado* (2003), and *Y todos éramos actores, un siglo de luz y sombra* (2016).

Some of his plays are: *El país de las lágrimas de sangre o nosotros te llamamos Chile libertad* (1978), *El huevo de Colón o Coca-Cola les ofrece un viaje de ensueños por América Latina* (1982), *Gonzalito o ayer supe que puedo volver* (1989), and *Cinco suspiros de eternidad* (1992).

After the military coup of 1973, Gustavo lived in France (1973-1985) as a political refugee where he recreated his theater group, Théâtre de la Résistance-Chili and performed in 17 international festivals, among them Avignon and Nancy. In 1985, after a failed attempt to return to his country, he was granted asylum in the Netherlands. He has lived in the US since 1992.

Forthcoming *Cómo quisiera / Longings and Brushstrokes / J'aimerais tant*, a trilingual Spanish, English and French poetry collection. He is the author of *Fragmentos*, a series of short videos in Spanish, conversations with the audience about the pathways to literary creation. He has been a guest writer/speaker at multiple professional conferences and is a regular contributor of opinion articles to Agencia Efe, and *Le Monde diplomatique*, Chile edition.

Andrea G. Labinger, professor emerita of Spanish at the University of La Verne, holds a PhD from Harvard and specializes in translating Latin American literature. Among the many authors she has translated are Sabina Berman, Carlos Cerda, Gustavo Gac-Artigas, Mempo Giardinelli, Ana María Shua, Alicia Steimberg, and Luisa Valenzuela. Three of her novel translations were finalists in the PEN Literary Competition.

In 2013, *World Literature Today* listed her translation of Liliana Heker's "The End of the Story" among the "75 notable translations of the year."

Gesell Dome, Labinger's translation of Guillermo Saccomanno's *Cámara Gesell*, was awarded a 2014 PEN/Heim Translation Fund grant. Published by Open Letter Books in 2016, the novel was a finalist for the Firecracker Award, sponsored by the Community of Literary Magazines and Presses.